CLAUDIA CRISTINA CORTEZ

UNCOMPLICATES YOUR LIFE

Advice
ABOUT SCHOOL

BY DIANA G. GALLAGHER

ILLUSTRATED BY BRANN GARVEY

STONE ARCH BOOKS
a capstone imprint

Claudia Cristina Cortez are published by Stone Arch Books
A Capstone Imprint
151 Good Counsel Drive, P.O. Box 669
Mankato, Minnesota 56002
www.capstonepub.com

Printed in the United States of America in Stevens Point, Wisconsin.
032013
007240R

Library of Congress Cataloging-in-Publication Data
Gallagher, Diana G.
  Advice about school: Claudia Cristina Cortez uncomplicates your life/
  by Diana G. Gallagher; illustrated by Brann Garvey.
    p. cm. — (Claudia Cristina Cortez)
  ISBN 978-1-4342-1905-3 (library binding)
  ISBN 978-1-4342-2252-7 (paperback)
  1. Middle school students—United States—Juvenile literature.
  2. Middle school students—United States—Conduct of life—Juvenile
  literature. I. Garvey, Brann. II. Title.
  LA229 .G26
    373.18—dc22   2009035124

ART DIRECTOR/GRAPHIC DESIGNER: Kay Fraser
PRODUCTION SPECIALIST: Michelle Biedscheid
PHOTO CREDITS: Delaney Photography

CLAUDIA

CAST OF

ME

CLAUDIA
That's me. I'm thirteen, and I'm in the seventh grade at Pine Tree Middle School. I live with my mom, my dad, and my brother, Jimmy. I have one cat, Ping-Ping. I like music, baseball, and hanging out with my friends.

MONICA is my very best friend. We met when we were really little, and we've been best friends ever since. I don't know what I'd do without her! Monica loves horses. In fact, when she grows up, she wants to be an Olympic rider!

MONICA

BECCA

BECCA is one of my closest friends. She lives next door to Monica. Becca is really, really smart. She gets good grades. She's also really good at art.

CHARACTERS

TOMMY's our class clown. Sometimes he's really funny, but sometimes he is just annoying. Becca has a crush on him . . . but I'd never tell.

TOMMY

PETER

I think **PETER** is probably the smartest person I've ever met. Seriously. He's even smarter than our teachers! He's also one of my friends. Which is lucky, because sometimes he helps me with homework.

ADAM and I met when we were in third grade. Now that we're teenagers, we don't spend as much time together as we did when we were kids, but he's always there for me when I need him. (Plus, he's the only person who wants to talk about baseball with me!)

ADAM

CAST OF

ANNA is the most popular girl at our school. Everyone wants to be friends with her. I think that's weird, because Anna can be really, really, really mean. I mostly try to stay away from her.

ANNA

NICK is my annoying seven-year-old neighbor. I get stuck babysitting him a lot. He likes to make me miserable. (Okay, he's not that bad ALL of the time . . . just most of the time.)

NICK

RANDI lives in Florida. She's in the same grade I am. She loves snorkeling, playing volleyball, and eating hot dogs. She and her brother, Mason, live in a house near the motel where my family is staying in Florida.

RANDI

CHARACTERS

Every school has a bully, and **JENNY** is ours. She's the tallest person in our class, and the meanest, too. She always threatens to stomp people. No one's ever seen her stomp anyone, but that doesn't mean it hasn't happened!

JENNY

CARLY

CARLY is Anna's best friend. She always tries to act exactly like Anna does. She even wears the exact same clothes. She's never really been mean to me, but she's never been nice to me either!

MASON is Randi's big brother. He's in eighth grade. He's really nice! He loves watching movies and playing dominoes. He told me that his favorite food is hamburgers. We have a lot of fun together!

MASON

INTRODUCTION

Every week, I spend about forty hours at *school*. That's as much time as my dad spends at his job. **SCHOOL IS SERIOUS BUSINESS**. And when you're thirteen, like me, school is the center of your **complicated life!**

School is where we see our friends, practice for sports, play instruments, rehearse plays, write newspaper articles . . . and a lot more. Plus, we go to classes, study, take tests, and turn in homework.

School is **SUPER IMPORTANT** to me and my friends. And it's not just because our future depends on it. It's because I spend so much time there.

This is your guide to **SURVIVING** middle school. I hope it makes your life a little less complicated!

▷ CHAPTER 1:
SCHOOL SAVVY
Get ready, get there, get organized

Quiz: What's your school style?

1. It's two weeks before the school year starts. YOU:

   a. plan **EXACTLY** what you're going to wear the entire first week, color-coordinate your school supplies, and taste-test lunch options.

   b. try to watch as MUCH TV as possible now. Once you have homework, you probably won't have much time. Oh, and you might pick up a few of the supplies you need, too.

   c. DON'T CHANGE A THING. There's still two weeks left of summer!

2. How much time do you need to get ready for school *every* morning?

   a. At least two hours.

   b. As long as there's time for a bowl of cereal, you're pretty much fine.

   c. You just wake up and head for the bus.

3. What's your **homework routine?**

    a. As soon as you get home, you finish EVERYTHING.

    b. You get it done sometime between getting home and class the next day. You don't stress about it.

    c. Homework? Were you assigned something?

4. How do you pick out what you're going to wear?

    a. Every week, you plan the next week's outfits.

    b. You think about it the night before, but **it's not a big deal.**

    c. You wear whatever's cleanest.

If you scored:

MOSTLY A'S: Your style is **overachiever**. It is good to work hard. But don't forget to have fun, too!

MOSTLY B'S: It sounds like you have a **good attitude** about school. But don't slack off!

MOSTLY C'S: You're laid back. Maybe too **laid back**. If you're falling behind, you know why.

It's the most important decision you'll make all day. It can make or break your day.

It can ruin your life!

I'm just kidding. It's not that big of a deal. But a lot of middle school girls *worry* about what to wear every day.

My favorite thing to wear is jeans and a t-shirt. I like being CASUAL and *comfortable*. Once in a while, I wear skirts. But most days, I'd rather be in my comfy jeans than worrying about my outfit.

Some girls worry too much about what to wear. They think people won't like them or will make fun of them if they wear an outfit that isn't fashionable.

I say they're wrong. I don't worry about what people think. I worry about how I feel. And I like to feel comfortable and casual.

That's how I dress for middle school success!

I AM
A
T-SHIRT

WHAT ABOUT UNIFORMS?

My school doesn't have uniforms. So I talked to my friends **Mason** and *Randi*, who I met on vacation in Florida. They have to wear uniforms to school, but they don't mind. They actually like it! Here's what they say:

You have to wear the same thing every day.

BUT . . .

YOU DON'T HAVE TO WORRY ABOUT WHAT TO WEAR.

....

You can't choose what you want to wear.

BUT . . .

YOU DON'T HAVE TO WORRY ABOUT HAVING EXPENSIVE CLOTHES.

....

You will look the same as your friends.

BUT . . .

YOU DON'T HAVE TO WORRY ABOUT FASHION.

THE WHEELS ON THE BUS

There are a lot of ways to get to school!

Walking — *Becca*, *Monica*, and I walk to school together every day. When it's really cold, one of our parents might drive us. I like walking to school. It gives me and my friends time to talk. Plus it's nice to spend some time outside.

Driven by a parent — Adam's mom works near our school. So every morning, she drives him to school. Then she picks him up after baseball or football practice.

TAKING THE BUS — TOMMY takes the bus to school every day. He says it's fun!

Driven by a sibling — Anna's big brother, **BEN**, drives her to school every day. I wish my brother could drive me sometimes, but he doesn't have a car.

RIDING A BIKE — PETER likes to ride his bike to school. He locks it up on a bike rack. If your school doesn't have a bike rack, this might not be a good idea.

In elementary school, we stayed in the same room most of the day. We just left the room for music, gym, and lunch. Now I have to walk all over the building to go to different classes. Check out my schedule:

8:00–8:15 — Homeroom: We hear morning announcements, take roll, and talk about upcoming events.

8:20–9:10 — First period: Math (I'm studying pre-algebra.)

9:15–10:05 — Second period: Biology

10:10–11:00 — Third period: Art

11:05–11:55 — Fourth period: History (My second-favorite class.)

12:00–12:30 — Lunch

12:35–1:25 — Fifth period: English (My favorite class.)

1:30–2:20 — Sixth period: Gym

2:25–3:15 — Seventh period: Study hall

EVERYTHING YOU NEED

One of the things I love to do every fall is shop for **school supplies!** Some schools send out lists of everything each student will need. Here's a list in case your school doesn't.

Claudia's School Supply List

- One **NOTEBOOK** for each class

- OR a three-ring **BINDER** with sections for each class

- At least **5** **pens** or pencils (depending on the rules at your school and which you like better)

- A pencil **SHARPENER**, if you prefer pencils

- One **FOLDER** for each class (or buy the kind of notebooks that have a built-in folder)

- Don't forget a **backpack**. Middle school kids get lots of homework!

LOVE YOUR LOCKER

Your locker is your home away from home. In elementary school, we had lockers. We only visited them before school, after school, and at lunchtime. In middle school, I go to my locker between classes, too. *That's about ten times a day!*

You keep your books, notebooks, and other supplies in your locker. **Here are a few more things to keep in your locker for emergencies:**

TISSUES

LIP BALM

EXTRA HAIR TIES

A COUPLE OF GRANOLA BARS

HAND SANITIZER

KEEP IT ORGANIZED

Because I keep so much stuff in my locker, I have to work hard to keep it **organized.**

I keep all of my books stacked on the bottom.

On the top shelf, I pile up all of my notebooks.  They are color-coded in RAINBOW order. I use red for my first class, orange for my second class, yellow for my third class, all the way to purple. That way, it's easy to remember what notebook I need to bring to class.

(*Roy G. Biv* = easy way to remember rainbow order. I skip indigo, since I don't need a notebook for gym class!)

My friends and I usually bring our backpacks to each class. I keep my pens and pencils and erasers and pencil sharpeners in my backpack. But I also keep backups in my locker. **WHO KNOWS?** All of my pens could run out of ink on the same day that all of my pencils get too short to sharpen!

LOCKER FLAIR

One of the best parts of having a locker is decorating it. Let your locker reflect your **personal style.**

You'll need:

- a stack of old fashion/gossip MAGAZINES

- **photos** of your friends, family, pets, crushes

- *tape*

- SCISSORS

- *extras*, like special magnetic pencil holders, mirrors, key hangers

Get your friends together. Everyone should bring magazines (that way, there will be more to choose from). Cut out pictures you like. Try famous people, cute animals, pretty landscapes, cool buildings, etc. Using tape, stick them to the inside of your locker. You can change the decorations in your locker **WHENEVER YOU WANT.** For fun, try doing it once a month to reflect that month's holidays or seasons!

▷ CHAPTER 2
FIRST RATE CLASSMATES:
Making friends & avoiding the bully

I'm **LUCKY**. I've had the same best friends since first grade. But what do you do if you're going to one middle school and your friends are going somewhere else? Or what if you're moving? **TRY THESE TIPS TO MAKE NEW FRIENDS.**

Find kids with similar interests

- Try joining a **club** at school. (Turn to page 65 for more information about clubs.)

- Pay attention. If you hear someone talking about a **MOVIE** you liked or a *book* you read, you can join the conversation.

- Speak up. Give your **HONEST OPINION** in class and when you're asked.

- If you have a hard time making friends at school, *don't give up*. You can find friends at church or synagogue, or by joining community groups.

Be brave

- Find a table of kids at lunch and ask if you can sit down. It might be hard to do, but you'll feel *great* afterward. (A good table has a group of kids who act like my friends and I do. Lots of laughing, talking, and smiling.)

- Try out for a SPORTS team, join the **choir**, or audition for a part in the school *play*.

Be friendly

- Put on a happy face, even if you're scared. SMILE at other kids. People will see that you're a friendly person.

- If you see someone who needs help, **HELP** them. By acting like a good friend even to a stranger, you're reaching out to someone.

Be yourself

- Don't pretend to be someone you're not. True friends will like the REAL YOU!

THE POPULAR CROWD

Lots of kids care about being popular. Not me. I've noticed that **no one really likes some of the most popular people** at my school. I'd rather have some really close friends than be popular. Luckily, I have FANTASTIC friends. I don't need to worry about being popular.

But sometimes it still hurts that I'm not in the popular crowd. When Monica tried out for the cheerleading squad, she started hanging out with the popular girls, like **Anna** and CARLY. That was hard. Anna and Carly usually aren't nice to my friends and me. So seeing Monica sitting at their lunch table wasn't fun at all!

But soon, Monica realized that she was happier hanging out with her old friends. Since then, we've all promised that no matter what, **we'll be friends.**

Even if one of us becomes "popular!"

Some things are more important than being popular, like:

- being a good **friend**

- being **KIND** to others

- trying hard, getting your homework done, and *doing your best* in school

- having your own **interests**

- **WORKING HARD** at things, whether you're good or not so good at them

- having **FUN** with your friends

- **BEING YOURSELF**

A note about being left out

Anna is always having parties that my friends and I aren't **invited** to. Once, I decided to throw a huge party and not invite her. But news travels fast in middle school, so she found out about my party. Then I felt bad. It hurt when she didn't invite me. And even though Anna is mean, I didn't want to hurt **HER** feelings. So I invited her. It was still fun.

THE TRUTH ABOUT BULLIES

Bullies are a fact of middle school life, just like locker combinations and mystery meat lunches. But that doesn't mean you have to be bullied. There are ways to avoid bullies. *Here are some of them.*

1. **IGNORE THEM.** (Recommended.) Bullies hate being ignored. At first, they might not leave you alone. But they'll get bored after a while. Then they'll stop bugging you.

2. BULLY BACK. (Not recommended!)

3. **TALK TO A TEACHER/PARENT ABOUT IT.** (Highly recommended.) You don't have to put up with bullying that makes you feel bad.

4. **Talk to your friends.** (Also highly recommended.) They might not be able to stop the bullying, but they'll help you feel better.

5. *Punch them.* (Not recommended **AT ALL**, even if my brother Jimmy says it's the best way.) You'll just get into trouble. And you don't want to become a bully yourself!

Not all bullies are mean to the core. In fact, when I had to work on a science project with **Jenny Pinski**, I found out the reason she became a bully.

I found out that in kindergarten, one kid teased Jenny so much that she stopped putting up with it. To get back at him, she teased him back. And it just kept going on like that. Any time Jenny thought someone was being **MEAN** to her, (even if they weren't really!) she was mean to them.

Pretty soon, Jenny was just mean to everyone. She didn't wait to see if other people were mean to her. She just decided everyone was mean. And now EVERYONE thinks Jenny is mean. I think even some of the teachers are scared of her.

The moral of the story? Bullies are people too. Maybe they're mean because someone else bullied them. That doesn't mean you shouldn't stand up for yourself. You should!

▷CHAPTER 3
IN CONTROL:
The people who run the school & make the rules

Classmates aren't the only people I see while I'm at school. There are lots of adults who help keep a school running.

Principal: Usually just one of these. Some schools have assistant principals or vice principals. The principal's job is to make sure the school runs smoothly.

He or she is the boss of the teachers. A principal is kind of like a king or queen. Or the President of the United States. The best principals really like kids. They listen to them, and they aren't mean. Our principal, Principal Paul, is really nice.

Teachers: Lots of these. There are a lot of different kinds of teachers. Everyone has their favorite.

Librarian: One of these, usually. The librarian works in the media center. Librarians order and arrange books. They're also really good at research. If you're ever writing a research paper, ask a librarian for help!

Teachers' aides/paraprofessionals: Many of these. They help the teachers.

Custodians: Anywhere from 1 to 25 custodians. It all depends on the size of your school. These people keep your school clean and comfortable.

Cafeteria workers: Like custodians, the number of cafeteria workers depends on how big your school is. Cafeteria workers prepare and serve lunch (and sometimes breakfast.) Then they clean up the dishes. There is usually one head chef in charge of planning all of the meals at a school.

Administrative assistants: These people work in the principal's office. They do paperwork, organize activities, and schedule appointments.

Guidance counselors: There may be one or more of these at your school. Guidance counselors talk to students about problems they are having. It might be a problem at home or one at school. They can also help students plan class schedules. And they help solve arguments between students.

Activities director: Usually, there's just one of these. This person is responsible for scheduling all of the activities at your school. He or she takes care of details like lining up officials for games or planning transportation to events.

Coaches: The number of coaches depends on the number of sports teams at your school. (Or one coach may be in charge of more than one team.) Coaches organize practices and teach players about the game. They encourage good sportsmanship and teamwork. At some schools, teachers act as coaches in addition to teaching their regular classes.

Band/choir director: There may be one or more band or choir directors at your school. (Some schools don't have any.) These people schedule practice for the band and choir and help musicians learn songs.

There might be other people who help keep your school busy and interesting. **You'd be surprised how many people it takes to run a school!**

TEACHER TYPES

Every school is different. But they all have one thing in common: teachers. To be a successful student, you need to know how to deal with many kinds of teachers.

AFTER ALL, THEY'RE THE ONES WHO GIVE YOU GRADES.

No two teachers are exactly the same, but there are a few common kinds. **Here's a handy guide:**

The Brain

This teacher is smart. Like, too smart. Way too smart. They know EVERYTHING. And they want to teach all of it to you.

GOOD THINGS: They have answers to all of your questions.

BAD THINGS: You can't ever fool them.

The Parent

This teacher really cares about you. They want to know how life is going, how you're feeling, if you're eating healthy lunches.

GOOD THINGS: They care!

BAD THINGS: You already have parents. You don't need more people prying into your private life.

The Pioneer

This teacher has taught at your school for about **three hundred years**. They have taught at your school so long, they know everything about everyone. They might have even taught one of your parents. Or grandparents.

GOOD THINGS: They might know secrets about your parents. (Like the time your dad got a D on a test. Or the time your mom threw up after eating too much Jell-O at lunch.)

BAD THINGS: They might remember things about you and tell your kids.

The Boss

This teacher likes things done a certain way. They don't want any excuses if you want to do things differently. Also, you must NEVER be late to class or ever break any rule. Ever.

GOOD THINGS: If they like you, they really like you.

BAD THINGS: If you mess up, they won't like you. And if they don't like you, watch out!

The Clown

This teacher is HILARIOUS! He or she knows lots of jokes and spends lots of time in class being funny and having fun.

GOOD THINGS: You always like going to class.

BAD THINGS: Sometimes you don't learn much. You're too busy laughing.

Remember this guide whenever you come across a teacher who you just can't figure out!

▷ CHAPTER 4
TOP OF THE CLASS:
Be your own best study buddy

It's **unavoidable**. If you're going to school, you're going to have to study. I usually have at least an hour of homework every night, and sometimes more!

I try to do my homework right away when I get home from school. That way, the rest of the night is free for me to do whatever I want. I even do that on Fridays. I want to be able to enjoy my weekend. And I can't enjoy it if I know I still have homework to do!

Got a big test coming up? *Here are some pre-test dos and don'ts:*

> **DO:** Study with a friend. You can help each other by making flash cards, quizzing each other, and talking about the things you don't understand.
>
> **DON'T:** Just pretend to study and goof off instead. Gossiping or reading magazines would be way more fun. But you won't learn anything!

DO: Take breaks from studying about once an hour.

DON'T: Take a break longer than 15 minutes. Your brain will get confused!

DO: Sleep. At least eight hours. Z Z Z Z

DON'T: Stay up all night studying. You'll be too tired to take the test!

DO: Look over your notes one last time before the test.

DON'T: Try to read the whole textbook before class.

DO: Eat breakfast the morning of the test. Your brain needs energy!

DON'T: Skip breakfast because you're too busy studying.

DO: Try hard. But if you don't know an answer, don't beat yourself up over it. You can try again next time.

DON'T: Cheat. What's the point?

Don't have all the answers? Need help studying?

Who should you ask for help?

• MOM/DAD/GRANDMA/GRANDPA/UNCLE/AUNT

Sure, it's been a hundred years since they were in school, but they might still remember the basics.

• OLDER BROTHER/SISTER

I don't like asking Jimmy for help unless I really need to. But in a pinch, he sometimes comes through for me. He even has some of his old notes from middle school to help me study.

• FRIENDS

Becca's great at science, but she's not great at math. So sometimes I help her when she doesn't understand something. And she helps me study for biology tests.

• THE INTERNET

Search "homework help" for some cool sites.

Sometimes, even when you study for hours, you might not understand your assignment. Don't be EMBARRASSED to ask a teacher for help. I mean, that's what they're there for!

Here's what you THINK will happen:

YOU: Mr. Teacher, could you help me with my algebra?

TEACHER: Ha-ha! You don't understand algebra? You must be stupid!

THE REST OF CLASS: Ha-ha! You're stupid!

That is NOT what will happen. Really. Trust me.

Wait until class is over. On your way out, stop and wait for everyone else to leave. Then:

YOU: Mr. Teacher. I've been having some trouble with algebra. Do you think you could help me?

TEACHER: OF COURSE! Come back at lunchtime and we'll go over it.

Trust me. Works every time.

1. Your teacher doesn't know your name.

2. There's half an inch of dust covering **EVERYTHING** in your locker.

3. The pages in your notebook only say the day's date, and don't have notes at all — just *doodles*.

4. You get every single question wrong on the test your class has been preparing for all semester.

5. Your parents sneak into your room and play books on tape while you sleep.

6. You forget how to count past 10.

7. You know **EXACTLY** how many ceiling tiles are in each classroom in your school.

8. When your parents asked what you did in school, and you say, "NOTHING," you're not lying.

9. You're a straight-F student.

10. **Nobody** would ever copy off your test, even if you paid them.

10 Signs You're Studying Too Hard

1. Your teacher assigns homework to the rest of the class. Then she tells you your homework is to take a night off.

2. You name your new dog Number 2 Pencil.

3. When you wake up in the morning, you realize that you were studying in your sleep.

4. Your mom *begs* you to watch some TV.

5. Your friends throw you a surprise party — in the **library.**

6. You haven't gotten a question wrong on a test in a year.

7. You find yourself mumbling times tables at the movies.

8. To FREAK you out, your sister tells you she noticed a pen leaking in your backpack.

9. Your best friend forgets your name.

10. School isn't fun anymore.

▷CHAPTER 5
LUNCHTIME!
The best time of the day

You might think the best part of the day is 3:15, when the bell rings and we all go home. But you're *wrong!* The best time of the day is 12:00. That's when we have lunch.

Lunch is by far the best part of the middle school day. It's when we get to **kick back** and RELAX with our friends. My friends and I gossip, talk, tell jokes, and laugh. A lot. If you're like me, you like being at school. But you don't feel like studying all the time. You need a break. That's where lunch comes in. It's a break from sitting in classes, working, and learning.

At my school, lunch is only half an hour long. *I wish it was two hours!* It would be really nice to have that much time to spend with my friends.

After we eat, we normally sit at our table and talk. Some people play basketball in the gym. When it's nice outside, our teachers sometimes let us go outside when we're done eating.

OUR FAVORITE LUNCHES

Tommy: *Pizza.* It's not as good as the kind at Pizza Palace, but it's still the best school lunch there is!

Adam: *Hamburgers.* I like mine with pickles, mustard, and ketchup. But no cheese.

Claudia: *Macaroni and cheese.* With brownies for dessert. Yum!

Monica: *Turkey and mashed potatoes.* We don't have it very often, but it's my favorite.

Becca: *Taco salad.* At our school, we can choose the toppings for our salads. I like lots of cheese and tomatoes, but not much meat and no onions.

Peter: *Ham and cheese sandwich.* It reminds me of the sandwich my mom makes when I stay home sick.

Jenny: I like **ANYTHING** that's good for food fights!

BROWN BAG BLUES

In elementary school, I used to bring my lunch **EVERY DAY**. My mom would pack a lunch for me every morning. It was usually a sandwich, a piece of fruit, and some crackers. I'd buy a carton of milk at school.

That got **boring!** By the time middle school rolled around, Mom was sick of making my lunch, and I was sick of eating it.

It was way more fun to have something different every day. Even if school lunch isn't the most delicious meal of my day, I don't mind.

Some people at my school do bring their own lunch every day. *Here are some great lunch ideas:*

SOUPS (in a thermos). Perfect for cold winter days or when you have a cold.

CRACKERS, CHEESE, AND AN APPLE. Apples go really well with cheddar cheese. Get a carton of milk or a bottle of juice to wash it all down.

MACARONI mixed with cut-up tomatoes and either shredded or fresh mozzarella.

BREAKFAST FOR LUNCH. Bring a bagel and cream cheese, plus orange juice. (Add some vegetables to make sure it's a balanced meal.)

HUMMUS WITH VEGGIES. Try carrots and sliced peppers. Add pita bread too.

SANDWICHES. Pack each piece of the sandwich separately, so nothing gets soggy. You'll need two slices of bread, but everything else is up to you! Here are some good combinations that will stay good even in your locker:

➤ **HAM AND CHEESE**

➤ **THANKSGIVING SANDWICH:** Turkey, mashed potatoes, stuffing, and cranberry sauce

➤ **BLT:** Bacon, lettuce, and tomato. (Hint: Slice the tomato before school. Then keep it in a separate container or baggie.) Add a little packet of mayonnaise if you like.

➤ **VEGGIE SANDWICH:** Lettuce, tomatoes, sprouts, green peppers, spinach, cucumber. Add onion if you want. This sandwich is really good with mustard or ranch dressing.

I try to eat healthy most of the time (although I love cookies and cake!). But I eat school lunches every day. Some people think that school lunches aren't healthy. I know better.

Even when you're eating school lunch, it's possible to be healthy.

Here's how:

- **Drink all of your milk.** Milk has calcium, which everyone needs. It also has protein, which gives you energy.

- **Eat your vegetables first**. That way, you'll make sure you get all the healthiest stuff first! You can fill up on vegetables and fruit, but make sure to eat some protein too.

- **Eat your dessert last.** If you're still hungry after you've eaten everything else, eat it. If not, give it to a friend!

- **Choose healthy options.** Eat salad instead of French fries, or baked chips instead of fried. (But once in a while, it's okay to have a treat!)

- **Don't starve yourself or skip meals.** When you skip a meal, your body thinks that it's being starved. That makes it hard for your body to process food right when you do eat.

- **Talk to your principal.** If your school lunches seem unhealthy, a bigger change is needed. Your principal can help you come up with a way to make lunches better for everyone!

A note about diets

If you're in middle school, you shouldn't be on a **diet** without talking to your doctor first. My doctor told me that if I ever want to go on a diet, I should talk to her to find out if I need to lose weight. If I am a healthy weight and get lots of activity, she said I don't need to diet.

If you think you're overweight, ask your mom or dad or school nurse for help. They can help you figure out a HEALTHY way to lose weight.

FRIENDS AND UNFRIENDS

Everybody knows that where you sit at lunch is probably more important than what you eat. After all, where you sit determines how much fun lunch is.

So where do you sit? It depends on who your friends are and if you're popular.

I don't care about being popular. ANNA and her friends do, so they pick the biggest table in the middle of the cafeteria. That way, everyone has to see them. They're **LOUD**, too, so that everyone has to hear them. To be honest, it can be pretty annoying sometimes for the rest of us.

My friends and I always sit together. It's always me, Monica, Becca, Adam, Tommy, and Peter. It's been like that since we started middle school.

Once in a while, someone else joins us. We **ALWAYS** include the new person in the conversation. I think our table is a really fun place to sit!

But not all of the tables in the cafeteria are fun. Once, when MONICA was trying out for cheerleading, she sat with Anna and her friends at lunch.

Monica acted like she was having fun, but she told me later that it wasn't fun at all. She and the other girls just had to sit and listen to Anna talk.

At our table, everybody talks to everybody else. *What's the point of just listening to one person?*

Our table is always OVERFLOWING with conversations, jokes, laughter, and happiness!

We:

- Tell **jokes** (Tommy can make any school lunch funny!)

- Talk about CLASSES

- **Help** each other with problems

- Plan FUN things to do on the weekends

- *Complain* about homework

- Study for TESTS

- *Have a great time!*

▷ CHAPTER 6
GET INVOLVED:
Finding the perfect extracurriculars

School isn't just about what happens in class or at lunch. All middle school students know that that's just the beginning.

We spend most of our time at school in class. But there's a lot more that goes on after — and sometimes, before — the bell rings. Most of my friends are in at least one EXTRACURRICULAR.

My Busy Friends

Peter: Science club, school newspaper, honor society

Tommy: School TV station, football

Adam: Every sport, band

Monica: Cooking club, photography club, riding lessons, band

Becca: Cooking club, theater, choir

Extracurriculars are good for you because:

- they're a great place to meet new people who have the same **INTERESTS** as you.

- they keep your mind **BUSY**.

- they help fill up your time, so you don't ever get **BORED**.

- you *learn* more things.

- they look great on **college applications.** Colleges want to know that you have lots of interests besides being a good student.

- you get more **EXERCISE**, since you're not sitting at home watching TV.

- they **HELP** other people (for example, being in a play helps entertain others).

- *they're fun!*

It is important to be involved with your school. But you don't want to overdo it. This quiz will help you see if you have the right balance.

1. You have a quiz coming up in your Spanish class. The night before, you:

a. *Panic!* You try to read your whole textbook, and fall asleep with it stuck to your face.

b. Try to stay **calm**. You go over your notes and go to bed early so that you're well-rested.

c. **GO OUT** with your friends, play video games, and watch a movie. Then you go to bed late.

2. It's *Homecoming*. How are you involved?

a. Cheerleading, trying for **Homecoming Queen**, decorating the float for the parade, baking brownies for the bake sale, chopping wood for the bonfire, and personally washing all of the football players' uniforms.

b. Supporting your team and going to the events you have time for. You don't go **OVERBOARD**, though. You still have homework, after all.

c. **WHAT'S HOMECOMING?**

3. Teachers refer to you as:

a. *Miss Do-It-All*

b. A GOOD student who tries hard

c. The one who **never** comes to class

4. What's your *favorite* part about school?

a. Everything!

b. One or two classes are really FUN, and your FRIENDS are there. You feel like you're learning a lot.

c. The minute it ends.

If you scored:

MOSTLY A'S: You need to **take it easy!** You might be spreading yourself too thin. If you're packing every second with activities, how do you have time to relax?

MOSTLY B'S: You're DOING GREAT! You are experiencing enough and having enough fun. And you're still doing well in your classes.

MOSTLY C'S: You need to *shape up!* School isn't important to you, and it shows. It doesn't have to be the most important thing in your life. But you do need to take it seriously.

MAKING MUSIC

There are two extracurricular options at my school that are MUSICAL: band and choir.

Becca loves to sing, so she is in the seventh grade choir. The group meets before school three days a week. They have concerts for holidays and at the end of the year.

Monica can't carry a tune, but she loves playing the flute. She started in fifth grade, and she has gotten really good! At our school, band meets three times a week during lunch. Monica doesn't like missing lunchtime fun with our friends, but she LOVES band.

The band performs at football and basketball games. They also march in the **HOMECOMING** parade every year. At holidays, they have a big concert. Lots of people in our town go.

Sometimes the band and choir get to travel to other towns to perform or compete against other schools. It's a really big deal when our band or choir wins.

PLAYING GAMES

The most popular extracurricular activity at our school — and, I bet, at a lot of other middle schools — is SPORTS.

I love sports, especially baseball. I don't play any at school, though, because I want to concentrate on my grades. But some of my friends play sports.

Brad Turino (my super secret crush!) is a football star. Adam plays football too. He also plays baseball. If Adam isn't busy with a game or practice, he's probably playing at home.

My other friends and I always try to see as many of Adam's games as we can. We all sit together. Sometimes we make signs to cheer Adam on. We always SCREAM and SHOUT and clap when he makes a pass or scores a run. After each game, we give him high-fives and hugs. We make sure to have a bottle of water for him so he can cool off and relax.

I know Adam loves having us there. Once he told me he always feels SPECIAL because he had his own fan club — us!

TRYOUT TIPS, BY ADAM

ADAM here, with my best tryout tips. Everybody knows that if you play sports, you have to stay in shape. But there's other stuff you should do if you want to make the team!

Drink lots of water. It's important to get lots of fluids. It helps your muscles work! You should drink at least eight glasses of water every day. You can also drink liquids like milk, fruit juices, and soda. But you shouldn't have too much juice or soda. All that sugar isn't good for you.

Practice at home — but not too much. You don't want to be too tired when you have to try out.

Warm up. Make sure to stretch before you do anything too tiring. Once you're all stretched out, start off slow by walking. Then start jogging, then running. That helps your body get used to exercising.

Be a good teammate. Coaches don't just look for good athletes. They also want players who will make a good team. That means being nice to other players. Don't hog the ball or try to be the star. Look out for other team members.

Eat right. Don't eat a bunch of candy the day of tryouts. Make sure to eat breakfast. Get both protein and carbohydrates. Carbs give you energy. Protein gives you strength.

My favorite tryout-day breakfast is eggs scrambled with broccoli and cheese. I have toast and a big glass of milk on the side. Have a healthy lunch at school. Then, after school, have a small snack. Try something like a granola bar and an apple. You'll be ready to go. After the tryouts, have a healthy dinner to make up for all the energy you burned!

Ask for help if you don't understand something. Once my basketball coach asked me to do something, and I didn't know what it meant. So I just pretended like I did. Pretty soon I realized I had screwed up. If I had asked what Coach meant, that wouldn't have happened!

Don't worry. If you don't make the team, keep practicing. You can try again next year!

Adam

Cheerleading Tips, by Anna Dunlap
(Most Popular Girl and Cheerleading Queen)

I like everyone to think that only the **PRETTIEST, most popular** girls are on the cheerleading squad. But really, that's not true. Anyone can be a great cheerleader.

Don't tell Claudia I told you this, but the **REAL SECRET** to being a cheerleader is just trying hard and having a good attitude.

A cheerleader should:

Be ready for hard work!

We practice every day after school and cheer for at least one game a week. That's a lot of activity.

Try and try again.

It takes a while to perfect every cheer. If I gave up after I tried the cheer once, it wouldn't be good!

Be happy — or be good at faking it.

We want fans to cheer with us, and no one wants to cheer with someone who's grumpy! Plus if we have big smiles on our faces, people are less likely to notice any mistakes we might make.

Take pride in her or his appearance.

Cheerleaders come in all shapes and sizes. But my friends and I try to make sure that our hair and makeup looks nice before the game starts. We wash our faces and brush our hair. It always looks best if our hair is pulled back and out of our faces.

Be a great leader!

After all, that's what cheerleaders are — leaders of cheers. We get other people excited and ready to watch the team win. And we support the players on the field or court.

Like I said, *anyone* can be a great cheerleader. It just takes a little work. Of course, *no one is as great as me.*

xoxo *Anna*

WHAT IF YOU DON'T LIKE SPORTS?

If you don't want to participate in sports at school, you can still stay active. Getting exercise is important, **no matter what.**

I get exercise by:

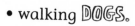

- walking DOGS.

- working in my mom's **GARDEN** or in neighbors' gardens.

- chasing my seven-year-old neighbor NICK.

- playing with my cat, *Ping-ping*.

- playing basketball in the driveway with my brother.

- batting practice with **ADAM.**

- putting on music and *dancing* with BECCA and **Monica** (or by myself in my room).

- going for **WALKS** with my grandma.

- riding my BIKE to run errands for my mom.

At our school, it's a pretty big deal to vote for class offices. Every student is expected to vote. After all, as Coach Johnson says, **"Democracy doesn't work unless people work for democracy."**

We have a class president, vice president, and secretary/treasurer. We also have student council, which includes three students from each homeroom.

- *President:* Goes to school board meetings, helps pass new rules, manages student council meetings

- *Vice president:* Goes to school board meetings when president is sick, goes to student council meetings

- *Secretary/treasurer:* Takes notes at student council meetings, keeps track of how much money the class has earned from fund-raising

- *Student council members:* Attend student council meetings, find out from other people in homeroom what the big issues are

When my friend PETER ran for class president,
I was his campaign manager. Here are some of
the things we did. (And it worked — Peter won!)

- **Make signs with funny slogans.** Peter's
  campaign posters were funny and true.

  He's not the coolest,
  But he's the smartest.
  Vote Peter for President,
  He's kind and honest!

  CAMPAIGN MANAGER
  Claudia

- **Be honest.** Don't run for president because you
  want to be popular or get things you want. Peter
  ran for president because he knew he was a good
  candidate and could help people. He was FAIR
  and HONEST.

- **Appeal to everybody.** Don't just try to get
  votes from the cool kids or the smart kids or
  the weird kids. If you want to win, all kinds of
  different kids have to vote for you.

- **Let the other candidates find out what your slogans are!** Anna was running for president too. She found out about Peter's slogans. Then she made up her own that were almost the same!

- **PANDER.** Pandering means making promises just to get people to vote for you. Peter refused to pander. Instead, he talked to Principal Paul about letting us wear T-shirts with words on them one Tuesday a month. Everyone loved the idea of T-shirt Tuesday. And Peter didn't have to make any promises he couldn't keep.

- *Buy votes.* Some of the other candidates gave away brownies, gumballs, and even signed pictures of themselves (Okay, I admit I wanted a signed picture of Brad). But Peter wanted people to vote for him because he had the best platform, not because he gave away the best treats. We just gave out stickers.

VOTE FOR PETER

Making a Speech

BY PETER WIGGINS, CLASS PRESIDENT

Did you know that most people are more afraid of talking in front of a big group than they are of dying? **It's true!**

I get really *nervous* making speeches. When I ran for class president, I had to make a speech in front of the whole school. It didn't go very well. But since I won, I've had to make a few more speeches. I've learned some TIPS to help make it easier to talk in front of people.

- **Practice in front of a mirror.** If you know your speech well, and you know how you look while you're making the speech, you'll feel much more confident.

- **Use note cards during your speech.** Write out your whole speech. Or if you want to sound more casual, just write down words to remind yourself of what you want to say.

- **Drink water before the speech** — but not too much. Before my first speech, I drank too much water because I was nervous and my throat was dry. It helped, but I had to go to the bathroom really, really bad!

- **Pick out one person to look at.** During my last speech, I looked at Claudia. Every time I saw her smile, I felt better and more comfortable. If you can't pick one person, try just looking right above the audience's heads. That way, it looks like you're looking at them, but you can focus on the back wall of the room.

- **Remember to smile.** If you don't, you might look like a grump. Then people won't want to listen to you.

- **Try to speak slowly and clearly.** Otherwise, people can't understand what you say.

- **Take a deep breath right before you begin.** You can do it!

Another thing people do at my school is work on the newspaper.

My school's newspaper is called the **Pinecone Press.** (That's because my school's name is Pine Tree Middle School.)

PINE CONE PRESS

Our newspaper started a couple of years ago. A student decided that we should have a newspaper and started one. If your school doesn't have a newspaper, *you could start one.* All you need to start one is a computer, a printer, and some people to help you. (You probably should also find out from your teacher or principal if it's okay if you start a newspaper!)

It takes a lot of people to put together a newspaper. **HERE ARE SOME OF THE DIFFERENT JOBS:**

Reporter: Reporters talk to other people to find out information. Then they turn the information into an article. Reporters should be **good at talking to others**, have computer skills, and be good writers.

Photographer: This person takes pictures to go along with articles. Photographers should have a good idea of what would make an interesting photograph. They should also be **friendly** and POLITE.

In the past, photographers had to know how to use a darkroom and special chemicals to develop photos. Now, photographers use digital cameras. Sometimes they also use special computer programs to make the photos look perfect.

Editor: This person decides what stories to put in the newspaper. They also assign reporters to write each article.

Once the articles are written, the editor reads them. They might make comments before the article is printed. Editors should be **GREAT READERS** and know about activities and events going on around school.

Proofreader: Proofreaders read articles to make sure that the spelling and grammar are correct. Proofreaders should have good grades in ENGLISH class and be **detail-oriented**. (Detail-oriented = someone who pays attention to the small things.)

At my school, there is also a teacher who advises the newspaper staff. English teachers are PERFECT for newspaper advisers. The teacher can help set up and print the paper. The teacher can also make sure there's a good place to work on the paper at school, so you don't have to work on it at someone else's house.

Here are some article ideas:

- *Sports:* A reporter should cover all the games, especially big ones. The reporter should find out what the score is and report about important plays that were made. They should also interview the star players.

- *School board:* Have a reporter attend school board meetings.

- *Interviews:* Interview important people at your school. But don't stop after interviewing the principal and the teachers. There are many more people worth interviewing! (Remember our list from page 26?)

- *Feature stories* on interesting students, like exchange students, new kids, honor roll students, sports stars, or just regular kids.

Being in a club is a GREAT way to meet people who have the same interests as you.

Here are some of the clubs at my school. Your school might have other clubs.

SPANISH CLUB: This club is made up of kids who like speaking Spanish. At their meetings, they speak only in Spanish.

PHOTOGRAPHY CLUB: This club goes on field trips to take photographs. They also use software to make their photos look really cool.

SCIENCE CLUB: This club gets together to do experiments. Once they almost blew up the science lab!

CHESS CLUB: This club meets to play chess. My friend Peter loves this club.

COOKING CLUB: This club cooks together. Once they made special treats for a party I had. They were really good!

DO YOU WANT TO DANCE?

One of the things that makes middle school different from elementary school is school dances. In elementary school, there were *no dances*. In middle school we have three a year. There is the seventh-grade dance, the winter dance, and Spring Fling! Dances are FUN, but they are also **STRESSFUL**.

You have to decide:

What to wear

Who to go with

Friends?

A date?

I was on the committee that planned our seventh-grade dance. At first, everyone was NERVOUS because we thought we all had to bring dates. And most of us aren't really ready for dating yet.

Then the boys decided they weren't going to go, because Anna wanted the dance to be a formal dance with ballroom dancing. When we decided to make our dance a contest, it became **A LOT** of fun for everybody.

Here's my advice about dances.

Dates: Don't worry about a date. Arrange for all of your friends to go together as a big group. That way you're guaranteed to have fun!

Flowers: Buy each other flowers. Or go to the florist together to pick out matching corsages.

What to wear: If you're not sure what to wear, ask your friends what they're wearing. If you want, you and your friends can wear dresses that go together. Everyone can choose a different dress in the same color family. Or everyone can wear a different color of the rainbow. Or you can all dress like characters in a favorite movie. There are TONS of fun possibilities!

Dancing: Most seventh-grade dances don't have ballroom dancing. At my seventh-grade dance we had to do special ballroom dances to earn points to win the challenge. So we practiced the dances in gym class first. You won't have to know how to WALTZ, TANGO, or JITTERBUG. You just have to move to the music!

DANCE TRADITIONS

Lady's Choice

An old-fashioned tradition, Lady's Choice is when a girl chooses a boy to dance with. At our seventh-grade dance, there were three Lady's Choice songs. Anna Dunlap snagged BRAD for two of them. But during the final song, Monica asked Brad to dance with me. (She said, "I'm a lady, and that's my choice.") **It was a really nice dance!**

Corsages and boutonnieres

Exchanging flowers is a SWEET-SMELLING dance tradition. It's always nice to give someone flowers when you're going on a date. But when you're dancing, you can't hold on to the flowers. That's where the **corsage** or *boutonniere* comes in. A corsage can be pinned to your dress or worn around your wrist with an elastic strap. A boutonniere is pinned to a boy's suit coat. The small flowers can either match your outfits or not.

Fancy dresses and tuxedoes

In the olden days, teenagers used to get really dressed up for every school dance. That's not always true now. Our school dance was fancy enough that I wore a **PRETTY** pink dress. But we also have some dances that don't require dresses for girls or special fancy clothes for guys. Find out what your friends are planning to wear if you're not sure.

Slow dancing

You don't need to know fancy ballroom dances to participate in a school dance. Usually, the music that's played will be music you know. No fancy jitterbug or waltz steps required. For a slow dance, you and your dance partner can just put your arms around each other — **like a relaxed hug** — and move in time to the music. Don't feel like you need to be really close together. Just be **COMFORTABLE!**

Limos

Save the fancy cars for prom!

▷ P.S.

Middle school is *different* from elementary school. But it doesn't have to be less fun! I've learned that if you **work hard**, you get to PLAY HARD too.

Middle school means more *freedom.*

More homework, but more **INTERESTING** classes.

More responsibilities, but more ACTIVITIES.

More **friends.**

More fun!

Claudia's Quick Tips for Middle School Success

- Get lots of SLEEP *zZzZZzz*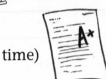

- Do **all** of your homework (on time)

- *Balance* fun and work

- Participate in **AT LEAST** one activity

- EAT RIGHT

- **Pay attention**

- Be **KIND** to others

- Try hard

- Do your **BEST**

- Be yourself

- *Have fun!*

ABOUT THE AUTHOR

Diana G. Gallagher lives in Florida with her husband and five dogs, four cats, and a CRANKY parrot. Her hobbies are gardening, garage sales, and grandchildren. She has been an English equitation instructor, a professional folk musician, and an artist. However, she had aspirations to be a professional writer at the age of twelve. She has written *dozens of books* for kids and young adults.

ABOUT THE ILLUSTRATOR

Brann Garvey lives in Minneapolis, Minnesota, with his wife, Keegan, their dog, Lola, and their very fat cat, Iggy. Brann graduated from Iowa State University with **A BACHELOR OF FINE ARTS DEGREE.** He later attended the Minneapolis College of Art and Design, where he studied illustration. In his free time, Brann enjoys being with his family and friends. *He brings his sketchbook everywhere he goes.*

GLOSSARY

boutonniere (boo-tuhn-EAR)—a flower worn by a man

casual (KAZH-oo-uhl)—ordinary or relaxed

complicated (KOM-pli-kay-tid)—difficult to understand

conversation (kon-vur-SAY-shuhn)—a talk between two or more people

determines (di-TUR-minz)—has an effect on

embarrassed (em-BARE-uhsst)—feeling uncomfortable and awkward

extracurricular (EK-struh-kuh-RIK-yu-lur)—referring to activities that are offered by a school outside of class

organized (OR-guh-nized)—arranged in a neat order

recommended (rek-uh-MEND-ed)—suggested as being good or helpful

responsible (ri-SPON-suh-buhl)—if someone is responsible for something, he or she has to do it

routine (roo-TEEN)—the regular way or pattern of doing things

schedules (SKEJ-oolz)—plans or timetables

surviving (sur-VIVE-ing)—continuing to go on

DISCUSSION QUESTIONS

1. What do you like to wear to school? Do you wear a uniform? Would you like to? Discuss how what you wear **impacts** your school day.

2. When you have a big test coming up, *how do you prepare?* Do you study a little all week? Do you cram the night before? How does your study method work for you?

3. What extracurricular activities do you do? Share something INTERESTING about the activity.

WRITING ACTIVITY

Pretend you are an **ADVICE COLUMNIST** for your favorite magazine. What advice would you give to solve these problems?

1. **HELP!** I have a fear of tests. Even though I always prepare, by the time the teacher passes out the exam, I am ready to pass out! How can I get a **grip** on my nerves?

2. I **HATE** lunchtime. All of my friends have a different schedule, so I don't have anyone to sit with. How can I make lunchtime *less lonely?*

3. I am on the yearbook, speech team, cheerleading squad, and have the lead in the school play. So I guess I'm pretty **busy**. My parents get upset with me because I am never home for dinner. I don't like fighting with them, but they don't understand that I have other commitments. **WHAT SHOULD I DO?**

STRAIGHT FROM TEENS

Here's what real teens, just like you, have to say about dealing with school.

I realize that homework is very boring and time consuming, but you have to do it. A good idea is to find a study partner so you can better understand the material you learn in school.

—Kenny, 16

Take it from the biggest procrastinator the world has ever seen. DO NOT PROCRASTINATE.

— Madeline, 15

READ UP
FOR MORE GREAT ADVICE!

☆ *For Girls Only: Wise Words, Good Advice*
by Carol Weston

☆ *Life Lists for Teens: Tips, Steps, Hints, and How-tos
for Growing Up, Getting Along, Learning, and Having
Fun* by Pamela Espeland

☆ *Middle School: The Real Deal, from Cafeteria Food to
Combination Locks* by Juliana Farrell and Beth Mayall

☆ *The Middle School Survival Guide* by Arlene Erlbach

☆ *Where's my stuff? The Ultimate Teen Organizing
Guide* by Samantha Moss with Lesley Schwartz

CLAUDIA
CRISTINA CORTEZ

WHATEVER
JOURNAL

MORE FUN
with Claudia!

When you're thirteen, like Claudia, life is complicated. Luckily, Claudia has lots of ways to cope with family, friends, school, work, and play. And she's sharing her advice with you! Read all of Claudia's advice books and uncomplicate your life.